W9-CBW-328

# Dear Parents:

Congratulations! Your child is taking the first steps on an exciting journey. The destination? Independent reading!

**STEP INTO READING®** will help your child get there. The program offers five steps to reading success. Each step includes fun stories and colorful art or photographs. In addition to original fiction and books with favorite characters, there are Step into Reading Non-Fiction Readers, Phonics Readers and Boxed Sets, Sticker Readers, and Comic Readers—a complete literacy program with something to interest every child.

## Learning to Read, Step by Step!

### Ready to Read    Preschool–Kindergarten
• big type and easy words • rhyme and rhythm • picture clues
For children who know the alphabet and are eager to begin reading.

### Reading with Help    Preschool–Grade 1
• basic vocabulary • short sentences • simple stories
For children who recognize familiar words and sound out new words with help.

### Reading on Your Own    Grades 1–3
• engaging characters • easy-to-follow plots • popular topics
For children who are ready to read on their own.

### Reading Paragraphs    Grades 2–3
• challenging vocabulary • short paragraphs • exciting stories
For newly independent readers who read simple sentences with confidence.

### Ready for Chapters    Grades 2–4
• chapters • longer paragraphs • full-color art
For children who want to take the plunge into chapter books but still like colorful pictures.

**STEP INTO READING®** is designed to give every child a successful reading experience. The grade levels are only guides; children will progress through the steps at their own speed, developing confidence in their reading.

Remember, a lifetime love of reading starts with a single step!

© 2021 DHX-Go Dog Go Productions Inc. Based on the book *Go, Dog. Go!* by P.D. Eastman
© P.A. Eastman Revocable Trust and Alan Eastman LLC.

All rights reserved. Published in the United States by Random House Children's Books,
a division of Penguin Random House LLC, 1745 Broadway, New York, NY 10019, and in Canada
by Penguin Random House Canada Limited, Toronto.

Step into Reading, Random House, and the Random House colophon are registered trademarks
of Penguin Random House LLC.

Visit us on the Web!
StepIntoReading.com
rhcbooks.com

Educators and librarians, for a variety of teaching tools, visit us at RHTeachersLibrarians.com

Library of Congress Cataloging-in-Publication Data is available upon request.

ISBN 978-0-593-30508-9 (trade) — ISBN 978-0-593-30509-6 (lib. bdg.)
ISBN 978-0-593-30510-2 (ebk)

Printed in the United States of America

10 9 8 7 6 5 4 3 2 1

Random House Children's Books supports the First Amendment and celebrates the right to read.

# Go, Dog. Go!

NETFLIX
A NETFLIX
ORIGINAL SERIES

## Welcome to Pawston!

by Elle Stephens

illustrated by Alan Batson

Based on the script

written by Adam Peltzman

Random House 🏠 New York

One morning,
Tag wakes up
her family.
It is very early!

Tag is too excited
to sleep.

There will be a party
in the tree today!

Tag gets her scooter.
She is ready
for the party
in the tree.

On the way,

she sees a moving truck.

She stops to meet

her new neighbor.

His name is Scooch.
He and his mom
just moved
to town.

"Welcome to Pawston!"

says Tag.

She invites Scooch

to the party in the tree.

Scooch's mom says yes.

Tag pushes a button.

A sidecar appears.

Scooch hops in!

Tag points
to the big tree.
That is where
the party will be!

Tag shows Scooch around
Pawston.
"Go, dogs. Go!"
she says.

They pass the ball store
and the doorbell store.

They see circus dogs!
One is Tag's sister,
Cheddar Biscuit.

Just then,

they stop.

It is a traffic jam!

There are so many dogs
going to the party!
There are dogs
on bikes and trikes.

There are dogs
in cars and trucks.
They are all stuck
in traffic.

Tag knows a shortcut!
She drives
through a hedge maze.

Then they get on a boat.

They meet

The Barkapellas.

They are singing dogs!

Oh no!

There is boat traffic.

Tag has an idea!

They get on a blimp.

The blimp flies
to the party.
But there is
blimp traffic, too!

Tag does not want

to wait in traffic.

They get off the blimp.

The party in the tree

is still so far away!

Dogs in cars and boats

and blimps are almost there.

"If we had waited,
we would have made it
to the party,"
says Tag.

Tag tells Scooch
she is sorry
he will miss the party.
But Scooch is not sorry.

Scooch had a fun day
riding in a car, a boat,
and a blimp.
And he made a new friend!

A dog named
Lady Lydia skis by.
"Do you like my hat?"
she asks.

"Yes!" Tag exclaims.

She has an idea.

Tag fixes the hat.

Now it can fly them

to the party!

It works!

Tag and Scooch finally get
to the party.

There are so many dogs!

Tag wants them all
to meet her new friend,
Scooch.

"Welcome to Pawston!"
they cheer.